THE UNICORN'S SECRET

#5

The Sunset Gates

by Kathleen Duey

illustrated by Omar Rayyan

ALADDIN

New York   London   Toronto   Sydney

For all the daydreamers . . .

ALADDIN

An imprint of Simon & Schuster Children's Publishing Division
1230 Avenue of the Americas, New York, New York 10020

This book is a work of fiction. Any references to historical events, real people, or real locales are used fictitiously. Other names, characters, places, and incidents are products of the author's imagination, and any resemblance to actual events or locales or persons, living or dead, is entirely coincidental.

ALADDIN is a trademark of Simon & Schuster, Inc.,
and related logo is a registered trademark of Simon & Schuster, Inc.
For information about special discounts for bulk purchases, please contact Simon
& Schuster Special Sales at 1-866-506-1949 or business@simonandschuster.com.
The Simon & Schuster Speakers Bureau can bring authors to your live event. For
more information or to book an event, contact the Simon & Schuster Speakers
Bureau at 1-866-248-3049 or visit our website at www.simonspeakers.com.

Book design by Debra Sfetsios
The text for this book is set in Golden Cockerel ITC.
Manufactured in the United States of America
0211 OFF
First Aladdin paperback edition December 2002
10 9 8
The Library of Congress Control Number for the Library Edition is 2002108388
ISBN 978-0-689-85346-3

✦

Wind whistles in the endless tall grass. The
Gypsies are traveling slowly. Heart is dressed
like one of them now, with a shawl and a
bright woven belt with tassels and tiny bells.
She walks beside a yellow caravan—
Moonsilver is inside it, safe, but restless.
Avamir and Kip follow closely. Dunraven's
forests are far behind Heart now. These wide
plains and the gray, stony mountains beyond
them belong to Lord Irmaedith.

✦

✦CHAPTER ONE

Heart squinted.

The sky arched deep blue overhead. It curved downward to meet the circle of the horizon.

There was a town in the distance.

The buildings looked tiny from here.

Heart called out to Davey. "Is that where we're going?"

He half-turned on the wagon bench and nodded. "Jordanville. We'll be there by tonight."

Heart shaded her eyes with one hand.

The buildings seemed to be standing at the edge of a sea of grass. The mountains beyond them made Heart smile. They had been traveling across the plains for a month. The land was as flat as a supper plate, and she didn't like it.

There had been no hills.

There had been no *trees*.

Moonsilver had been free to graze only at night.

Inside the painted wagon, Moonsilver stamped his forehoof. It was a hollow, impatient sound. He hated being cooped up, Heart knew. But there was no choice.

Moonsilver's white coat made him all too easy to see here. His beautiful horn was impossible to hide.

"We'll be in the mountains before long," she said in a soothing voice. "You'll be able to get out of the wagon more often."

Heart glanced at the rocky peaks beyond the distant town. They looked gray, not green.

Heart sighed. Binney had said there were forests farther on. But how much farther? Beyond the mountains?

Moonsilver stamped again.

Heart pushed up her sleeve and twisted the braided silver bracelet on her wrist.

Mountains would be better than plains, but thick forests were best.

It was so hard to keep the unicorn colt hidden.

Would he ever be able to run free?

Heart looked at the long line of Gypsy wagons. Binney's bright blue one led the way. Heart's carry-sack and blankets were in it.

Talia's family came next. Their wagon was patterned green and silver. Then came Davey's cousins with their apple red wagon, then Davey's parents and Josepha's older brother and his wife.

Each wagon was like a flower—bright, different from all the rest. Gypsies were like that, Heart thought—their clothes, their hair, their wagons—each person was different and lovely.

The horses that weren't harnessed walked alongside the caravan of Gypsies, grazing as they went.

Some had halters, but most wore no tack at all.

Sometimes Heart played at teaching Kip and Sadie to be herd dogs, but the horses needed little guidance. They were used to keeping pace with the wagons.

Heart frowned. It was so unfair that Moonsilver had to ride inside a stuffy caravan.

The stone-colored mountains in the distance reminded Heart of the mountains she dreamed about so often. She straightened her shoulders. She had to find her family somehow. The book she'd found in Lord Dunraven's castle might help.

"If I can ever learn to read it," she whispered to the sky. Then she sighed.

The woman she'd met in Yolen's Crossing had said it took weeks to learn the letters. The Gypsies never stayed anywhere longer than a day or two.

Heart kicked at a pebble.

Kip whined softly and looked up at her.

Heart patted him. He swung his tail from side to side.

"I'm tired of hiding and worrying," Heart told him.

Behind her, Avamir shook her mane.

Heart turned to face the unicorn mare.

Avamir reached out, blowing a warm breath along Heart's cheek. Heart kissed the mare's scarred forehead.

"If I can find my family," she said quietly, "they will help us."

Avamir switched her tail.

"They will," Heart said, as if the mare had disagreed with her.

But Heart knew she couldn't be sure.

It didn't matter how much she wanted it to be true.

Whoever her parents had been, they had left her by the river in Ash Grove.

They had never come back to find her.

Maybe they had left her because they just didn't want her.

Heart flinched away from the thought, as always.

She laid her hand on Kip's head.

Her eyes stung. She squeezed them shut.

This was no time to cry.

She had to worry about Moonsilver and Avamir and Kip now, not about herself.

Inside the caravan, Moonsilver struck his hoof against the planks again.

"Play your flute for a while," Davey called over his shoulder. "It calms him down."

Heart pulled her flute out of the shoulder-case Zim had made for her.

She was lifting it to her lips when she noticed tiny, dark shapes on the horizon.

For a long moment she stared, blinking.

Then she lowered the flute.

They hadn't run into anyone since they had wound their way down out of Dunraven's mountains.

"See the riders?" Davey asked.

"Yes," Heart answered.

The riders were separating, fanning out. Heart watched, puzzled and scared. Why would they do that?

"Guardsmen," Davey said. "Lord Irmaedith's."

Heart stared, wondering how he knew.

Then she saw a flash of reflected sunlight. Only silvered steel sparkled like that; it was their sword scabbards.

"What do they want?" Heart asked.

"Keep your wits," Binney called out, her clear voice carrying down the line of wagons. "They just want to see what we're about, same as always."

Heart swallowed hard.

She could hear the hoofbeats now. In a few moments the guardsmen would be upon them.

✦CHAPTER TWO

The hoofbeats got louder as the riders galloped closer.

The tall grass hid the horses' legs and they seemed to fly across the ground.

"Be quiet and calm," Binney said. "I'll talk to them."

Avamir nickered.

Moonsilver answered from inside Zim's wagon.

"Be still, Moonsilver!" Heart pleaded, glancing at the approaching riders. There were ten or more of them, all dressed in dark shirts, all riding bays and blacks. Even their saddles were dark leather.

"Lord Irmaedith must want them to look fierce," Heart said just loudly enough for Davey to hear.

Then she pressed her lips together.

The riders were close, pulling back on their reins. The horses plunged and reared, sliding to a stop.

"By what right do you pass here?" a deep voice demanded.

Heart's whole body went tense.

No one answered.

Kip whined a little and Heart saw that the hair along his back was rising. She patted him, trying to soothe him into silence.

Sadie growled once and Josepha picked her up.

Then there was only the sound of the wind. Binney walked toward the rider who had spoken.

"We travel by an ancient right," she said clearly as she got closer. "We travel with the permission of the wind and the sky and the dust."

The rider scowled at her a moment, then grinned. "Well said." He frowned. "I know you, I think, old woman."

"I am not so old I can't recognize a boy grown up."

The man laughed. "You can't possibly remember me."

Binney nodded. "You once begged me to let you see the show for free. Your father wouldn't pay your way in."

The man shook his head in disbelief. "You're just guessing. You—"

Binney smiled. "It was that dusty little place straight east of Salzberg on the old pike."

The man burst out laughing. "And you let me in!"

Binney smiled. "You must have charmed me."

Heart's breath released itself in a soft sigh.

Binney was amazing.

These men didn't seem so dangerous now.

Most of them were smiling.

Now if they would just leave soon . . .

"I wanted to join your show," the man said.

"Did you?" Binney said. "I am sure I said no."

The man nodded. "You said boys should not leave their mothers too young."

Binney nodded. "I still believe that."

"We found one this morning," the rider said. "He won't tell us what he's up to." The man lifted one arm to point.

Heart followed his gesture.

One of the riders had a boy riding behind him.

As Heart watched, the horse sidled, uneasy among the Gypsy wagons. As it turned, Heart saw the boy's face.

She bit her lip.

Tibbs? Tibbs *Renner*? What was he doing here?

Heart stepped back so that he wouldn't see her.

Her spirits sank.

Tibbs had recognized her with the Gypsies in Derrytown.

She had heard him telling people that Moonsilver was a real unicorn. She had run away, afraid people would believe him. Had he been following her when the riders caught him?

"We've heard rumors about unicorns," the rider said.

Heart's thoughts scattered like startled sparrows. She held her breath.

Binney laughed easily.

She gestured at Avamir. "There's the mare we use. She isn't wearing her goat's horn just now."

Avamir raised her head high as if she understood.

Her forehead was stained from the pine gum they used to attach the goat horn.

The rider laughed. "Very clever. Where are you going?" he asked Binney.

"Jordanville," she said. "Then along the high road on to Lord Levin's domain. We always pay our town fees," she added.

Heart peeked out at Tibbs. He was staring at the sky.

"What'll you do with the boy?" Binney asked.

The rider turned. "Why? Do you know him?"

Binney shrugged. "No. Has he stolen something? Is he in trouble?"

The rider shrugged. "Maybe. Derrytown apprentice-boys run away on this road. Lord Irmaedith expects us to turn them back."

Binney was so kindhearted. Heart knew she wanted to help Tibbs.

Heart watched, uneasy. Tibbs had been apprenticed to a blacksmith in Derrytown. That meant he had signed an agreement to work for four years without pay.

It was fair.

Apprentices learned a good trade during their four-year term. The trade masters were paid for all their teaching by four years of the boys' work.

It was a solemn agreement. Apprentices weren't *allowed* to leave until their four years were up.

Heart frowned.

Whether he had run away or left with permission, one thing was sure.

Tibbs wasn't going home. Ash Grove lay in the opposite direction.

Binney turned and caught Heart's eye, her eyebrows arched.

Heart shook her head slightly, pleading with her eyes.

Binney sighed.

She turned back to face the rider.

"We really haven't any use for another boy, I am afraid," she said. "Though he looks honest enough to me."

Heart saw Tibbs eyes widen. He hadn't expected Binney to be kind.

"He'll be honest soon," the rider said. He laughed. "A night or two in with the thieves and the fleas and he'll be eager to tell us his plans."

Without warning, Tibbs slid sideways, tumbling off the horse. He hit the ground running.

✦CHAPTER THREE

Tibbs had startled everyone. At first the riders didn't react. Sprinting, Tibbs stumbled, then righted himself.

Heart watched, amazed. Tibbs had to be scared witless. He had no chance of getting away—he couldn't possibly expect to outrun horses.

At that instant, Tibbs swerved sharply and headed for the line of wagons. Before anyone could stop him, he had made his way through and was floundering in the tall grass on the other side.

The wagons were close together, with children and old people standing between them.

The riders reined in, furious.

They couldn't get through.

The man Binney had been talking to began shouting orders.

The riders split into two groups. They galloped in opposite directions, riding along the line of wagons.

Heart turned around to watch Tibbs.

He had slowed down; the grass made it hard to run.

Heart glanced at the riders. They would gallop to the ends of the wagon line, then turn and race toward Tibbs.

He would be surrounded in seconds.

As if he had heard her thoughts, Tibbs stopped. He turned and saw what the riders were doing. He looked around wildly, then ran back toward the wagons.

Heart stared.

He was coming straight toward her.

She knew that a commotion close to the wagon might panic Moonsilver. The riders would hear him stamping and kicking.

They would wonder why he was hidden inside a caravan.

They might insist on looking inside.

And if they did . . .

Heart lifted her shawl to make a loose hood around her face, then stepped out from behind the wagon. "Kip?"

The dog yipped in response.

"Turn him," Heart said, using the herd-dog command she had taught Kip. "Get him!"

She gestured at Tibbs.

Kip leaped out, barking wildly, baring his teeth.

It worked.

Tibbs veered away, dodging through the little herd of loose horses, startling them into trotting a few steps. Avamir reared as Tibbs passed, making the riders' horses shy.

Kip stayed close to Tibbs's heels, barking and snarling.

Tibbs sprinted, his legs blurred by the tall grass.

As Heart watched he turned sharply once more, then stumbled and fell, sprawling flat.

As the guards spurred their horses forward, he rolled over, flinging his right arm out as he scrambled to his feet.

Then he ran again, heading straight away from the road.

When the riders caught up with him, he stopped.

He stood still as they circled him.

He didn't answer their angry shouting.

He did not try to run again.

Heart called Kip back.

He barked once, then sat, panting, pressing against her leg.

The men got Tibbs up on a horse. One rider shook his fist, scowling.

Tibbs hung his head, looking scared. He didn't even glance back toward the Gypsy wagons.

Heart was pretty sure he hadn't noticed her.

She hoped desperately that he would think she wasn't with the Gypsies any longer.

The guards reined their horses around.

The rider who had talked to Binney waved.

"My thanks, old woman, for that free show when I was a boy. I'll repay you one day!" he shouted.

Binney waved back as the men galloped away.

Heart stared after them. What would they do to Tibbs?

Binney walked toward her, frowning. "You know the boy." It was not a question.

Heart nodded. "From Ash Grove. He was always mean to me." She sighed. "He saw the Derrytown show when Moonsilver saved Davey. I overheard him telling people Moonsilver was real. That's why I ran away."

Binney's face hardened. She smoothed Heart's hair. "Don't worry. He won't cause you trouble. He has enough of his own to keep him busy."

Settled back on the driver's bench of her wagon, Binney raised one hand and signaled the drivers to start.

Heart fell into her place beside Moonsilver's wagon.

Davey began to whistle quietly as they started off.

Heart glanced back along the wagon line.

Josepha and Talia were practicing dance steps, walking alongside Josepha's family.

The sound of Zim's flute began.

Heart stared at the flattened grass where Tibbs had fallen.

A quick, warm squeeze on her wrist startled her into gasping. She pushed back her sleeve.

It had felt like the braided silver thread of her bracelet had tightened for a second, then loosened again.

Heart stared into the tall grass, remembering the way Tibbs had flung his arm outward. He had *thrown* something.

Heart drew in a quick breath. It all made sense.

Tibbs hadn't really expected to escape.

He had mostly wanted to hide something from the riders.

But what?

Heart walked closer to the patch of flattened grass, scanning the ground.

There! There *was* something in the grass.

Heart looked back at Davey. He was staring straight ahead.

She glanced down the line of wagons. No one was watching.

It was a book—a small, dirty, and tattered one.

Heart scooped it up and tucked it into her dress pocket.

Then she called Kip and dropped back to walk beside Moonsilver's wagon again.

After a few minutes Heart pulled the book from her pocket.

If only she could read!

She held it close to her chest and flipped through the pages. There were not as many words in this one. There were dozens of drawings.

There were spirals and curves and complicated shapes. There were silhouettes of eagles and bears and . . .

Heart stared. The lines were clear and dark, like the design in the book from Lord Dunraven's castle. The drawing was of two rearing unicorns, facing each other. Behind them was a setting sun.

It was *exactly* like the drawing in Dunraven's book. It was the same design as the one on the blanket she'd been wrapped in when Simon Pratt found her.

Heart was so startled, she dropped the book.

She bent to pick it up.

Trembling, she put the book back into her pocket.

✦CHAPTER FOUR

Jordanville had clean, wide streets. The buildings were made of white stone laid in rows like
giant bricks.

The Gypsies set up camp on a wide, grassy
place outside town.

Heart helped light the circle of lanterns for
the show. The townspeople sat quietly while they
waited.

When the show started, Binney made them
laugh at her jokes.

Zim and Heart played their flutes for Josepha
and Talia's lovely dance.

The audience sighed.

They applauded for a long time.

They loved the jugglers.

They shouted and clapped after the children did their acrobatic tricks.

And when Avamir appeared out of the darkness with the goat's horn stuck on her forehead the audience made a sound like wind sighing through pine trees.

Heart had changed the act a little. Davey had gotten good at falling off the high wire, so they had raised it a little.

The audience gasped when he fell. Heart was always amazed at how much the act looked like a terrible accident.

Heart began to play the soft, sad melody on the flute that brought Avamir galloping from the shadows beyond the lantern light.

Her hoofbeats shook the ground as she circled.

She plunged to a stop, rearing. Then she slowly lowered the goat horn to touch Davey's lips.

Davey opened his eyes as though a unicorn had healed him—just like in all the old stories. He stood up slowly, then bowed.

Avamir extended one foreleg to bow beside him.

The audience loved it.

They stood up to clap and shout.

Binney smiled and thanked them, then bid them good night.

Zim and Heart played softly as the people left.

Once the lanterns were out, Heart got her carry-sack out of Binney's wagon.

"Sleeping outside?" Binney asked.

Heart nodded. "It's not too chilly, and I hate being apart from Moonsilver."

Binney smiled, holding the candle lantern high so that Heart could see her face. "I'll feel easier when we are on the road and alone again too."

Binney climbed into her wagon, then came back down the little ladder, holding a folded blanket. "Take an extra. Keep Kip close."

Heart thanked her. "I'll let Moonsilver out for a while before I sleep," she added.

Binney nodded. "Don't go far from the wagons."

"I won't," Heart promised.

She walked back down the long line of wagons.

The stars glittered overhead.

She let Moonsilver out. He shook his mane and trotted back and forth for a few minutes. Then he settled in and grazed beside his mother.

Once he had eaten he cantered across the field in the dark.

A moment later he came back, tossing his head.

It had scared Heart at first, letting him gallop around at night.

But he never stumbled. It seemed as if he could see perfectly in the dark.

His hooves made less noise than a horse's. It was as though his whole weight never quite struck the ground.

Once Moonsilver was safely back inside the wagon to sleep, Heart kissed Avamir's muzzle. The warm grass-smell of the mare's breath tickled Heart's nose.

"Good night," Heart said. Avamir touched her cheek, then paced away to stand close to the wagon. She lowered her head.

Kip turned three circles.

He lay down beside the wagon wheel.

Heart smiled.

No one would be able to get near the wagon without Kip and Avamir sounding an alarm. Moonsilver was safe for the night.

She stretched and yawned. The grass smelled clean and damp as she knelt to feel for her carry-sack.

She pulled out a candle and Tibbs's book, then turned back the blanket. She hesitated, listening. Footsteps?

"Ssst!"

Heart slid the book into her pocket. "Who's there?"

It had to be Davey or Talia or Josepha.

But no one spoke. No one stepped out of the darkness.

Heart shook her head. She had imagined the sound.

Then it came again.

"Pssssst! Heart?"

It was a rough whisper.

Kip stood up and faced the voice. He growled.

"No tricks, Davey," she said quietly, feeling her stomach tighten a little. The moon was low and dim, and she couldn't see anything by the light of the stars.

"Heart?"

"Who is it?" she demanded, feeling her pulse quicken, afraid she knew the answer to her own question.

Kip tilted his head, baring his teeth.

The whisper came again. "It's me. Tibbs. Call the dog off, Heart. I just want to talk."

Heart rested one hand on Kip's back. Had Tibbs seen Moonsilver grazing? Her pulse fluttered in her temples like bird's wings. She glanced at the wagons.

No one was stirring.

"Hush, Kip," she said quietly. Then she lifted her chin. "If this is some wicked trick, Kip will raise an alarm and—"

"No need for threats, Heart," Tibbs said. "I came to beg your help."

He stepped forward. Heart tried to see his face.

Even this close the darkness blurred his features.

"I know the unicorn is real," he added, lowering his voice to a whisper again.

Heart bit her lip. "We stick the horn to Avamir's forehead with pine gum—," she began.

"The colt in the wagon still has his own horn," Tibbs said. "I saw him." He sighed. "No one in Derrytown believed me."

"Some did," Heart told him. "The guards have followed us and—" She stopped, blinking back tears. "Why do you hate me, Tibbs?"

"I don't," he said quickly. "Not anymore. Ruth Oakes was my only friend. And then it seemed you were always with her and I . . . I . . ." Tibbs's voice stalled.

"Why should I trust you?" Heart demanded.

Tibbs looked up at the stars, then back at her. "Heart, if I travel alone, the guardsmen will find me. They ordered me back to Derrytown." He grimaced. "I had my master's permission to leave."

Heart frowned. "Why would he give you permission?"

Tibbs hesitated. Heart could hear him breathing. "He knew why I wanted to come."

Heart waited, but he said no more.

She smoothed her dress.

Her hand bumped the edge of the book in her pocket. She traced its shape with her fingers. "Can you read, Tibbs?"

"Yes," he said, "and write. Apprentices have to learn."

Heart set her jaw. "Teach me to read, and promise to keep the unicorns secret. I will ask Binney to let you come with us."

"Agreed," Tibbs said solemnly. "I give you my word, Heart."

Heart pulled the book from her pocket. "Here," she said, "I found this in the grass."

Tibbs reached out. He gasped when he realized what she was handing him.

Heart leaned toward him to whisper. "What are the drawings?"

"Metalwork designs," he whispered back.

Heart tilted her head. "Fancy iron fences and gates?"

"Yes," Tibbs said, excited. "And amazing castle doors, beautiful suits of armor . . . all designed and made by the best smith who ever lived."

Heart closed her eyes. Metalwork? It made no sense. Why would the embroidery design from her baby blanket match a drawing in both Dunraven's book and Tibbs's?

"Why did you throw it?" Heart asked him.

He let out a breath. "The book is the reason my master let me come. I bought it from a Derrytown junkman."

Heart waited in silence until he went on.

"My master wept when he saw it. He longs to meet the man who made these designs. All smiths do."

Heart frowned, then realized he couldn't see her in the darkness. "Because he is so good?"

"Yes," Tibbs told her.

"You should have shown the book to the guards," Heart began. "They must know—"

"They would have never let me out of lock-up," Tibbs said simply, interrupting her. "That's why I threw it. Lord Irmaedith claims the smith doesn't exist."

Heart shook her head, puzzled. "Why?"

"So that no other lord will have swords and armor as fine as his."

+CHAPTER FIVE

Binney welcomed Tibbs when Heart asked.

She made him vow he would keep the unicorns secret.

Tibbs looked solemn and sure when he promised.

Heart didn't quite trust him. She wasn't sure if she ever would. But as the days passed she decided Ruth Oakes had been right.

Tibbs's father had been *so* mean.

All the yelling and punishment had made Tibbs mean, too.

But Tibbs's apprenticeship had helped him.

His master had been good to him.

And the Gypsies were kind to him too.

Tibbs was polite now.

He didn't tease anyone.

He helped people.

Amazingly Kip liked him right off. Avamir didn't seem to mind him either. Moonsilver was shy, but he was that way around almost everyone.

Tibbs kept his word about teaching her to read and write.

He gave her lessons every night. He showed her how to write the alphabet. He taught her the sounds the letters made.

They sat with their backs to the fire so the light would fall on Tibbs's papers.

The Gypsy children sat close, listening.

Zim would move closer too. He already knew some of the sounds.

Tibbs knew them all.

"H-H-i-i-lll . . . hill!" Heart said one evening. "The word is 'hill'!"

"Good," Tibbs said. He smiled. He pointed at the next word he had written.

Heart stared at it. The first two letters were the same as the last word. "H-H-Hit," she said. "Hit!"

Tibbs grinned.

Heart felt puffed up and proud, like a strutting rooster.

She laughed. "I read! I read two words!"

Tibbs pointed at the next word. By the end of the evening she had sounded out many more.

"What town are you looking for?" Heart asked Tibbs the next day as they walked along the narrow road. Zim was playing a lively tune on his flute. Several of the girls were singing.

"I'm not sure," he told her. "I don't know the man's name. No one does. Some say it's just a tale."

He looked into Heart's eyes and spoke quietly. "I was born to work metal, Heart." He turned away. "I know that sounds silly."

"Not to me," Heart told him.

That night, Heart let Moonsilver out.

He galloped over the rough rocky ground.

She looked up at the moon, listening to Moonsilver's swift, light hoofbeats and thinking about her own life.

She loved playing her flute, but not like Zim did. Music was the most important thing in his life.

Ruth Oakes loved healing people, helping anyone sick or hurt. That was her purpose.

Heart sighed.

What was *her* purpose?

She opened the caravan doors when Moonsilver was ready to sleep.

Then she went to Binney's wagon and slid into her blankets.

That night she dreamed about the moon-colored mountains again. In the dream she was running uphill, leaping from one huge rock to the next.

When she woke the silver bracelet felt tight. She pushed it down onto her wrist and blinked in the gray dawn light.

Kip whined outside the wagon.

Heart rubbed her eyes.

She sat up.

Binney was still sound asleep.

Heart pulled Lord Dunraven's book from her carry-sack and opened it.

Most of the words were not simple like "hill" and "hit" and "run" and "hop."

She couldn't read it.

Not yet.

Heart put the book away and climbed down out of the wagon.

Kip jumped up. He ran in tight circles around her. He acted as though she had been gone a long time and he had missed her.

That day and the next, the wagons wound along a narrow mountain road.

There were rocks piled waist-high along the road in some places.

Every traveler picked up a few more and helped keep the road clear enough for wagons.

The nights grew colder.

The Gypsy children huddled around the fire every night, chanting the letter sounds along with Heart.

Tibbs's lessons got longer and longer. Binney bought big sheets of paper in a town they passed through.

Tibbs wrote words for the children to sound out. They learned to say the vowels.

Heart led them, almost singing. "Aaaaa, Eeeee, Iiiii, Ooooo, Uuuuu . . ." Her breath hung in wispy clouds in the still, cold air.

One afternoon, the wagons rounded a long bend.

"This is Thoren," Davey said, turning on the driver's bench. "There's a surprise in this town for you." He grinned and faced forward again.

Heart looked around, wide-eyed. Thoren? A town?

But there was no town, just boulders as big as barns jutting up out of the ground.

Then Heart noticed the stone walls that had been built between some of the boulders.

The houses weren't square. They weren't round or any other regular shape.

Each one was different.

The doors were round, though. Each was painted a soft color that nearly matched the rock that surrounded it.

Heart was sure that people had ridden through Thoren in the dusk of twilight many times and had not noticed it was there at all.

"This town has more books than you've ever seen," Davey said.

Heart smiled at him. He was learning to read too.

They all were.

"Where?" Heart called back, running a few steps to catch up. She grinned, sure he was teasing. Books were rare.

"Just up here," he answered.

Heart walked close to the driver's bench.

"There!" Davey said, pointing.

Heart peered at one of the strange stone buildings. The wide doors were open. The slanted afternoon sun shone inside.

Heart blinked. There were hundreds of books inside, stacked neatly on wooden shelves.

Davey laughed. "You thought I was making it up, didn't you?"

Heart nodded, still staring.

As she watched a woman came out of the building. She swung an iron gate open and Heart gasped.

Davey turned to grin at her again.

She glanced at him, then back at the gate.

Beautiful figures were worked into the dark metal: two rearing unicorns, with a setting sun between them.

"Thank you!" Heart said to Davey.

He smiled.

Heart knew he thought she was excited about the books and she *was*. But she was astounded by the gates and she couldn't explain. She had never shown Dunraven's book to anyone but Zim.

Heart blew Davey a kiss and he laughed. Then she whirled around and ran down the line of wagons.

Kip followed at her heels, bounding along.

When she found Tibbs, she pulled him to the side of the road. She pointed at the iron gates.

A look of wonder came into his eyes.

✦CHAPTER SIX

Binney guided them straight through town as usual.

They set up camp in a little meadow framed by huge boulders and tall pine trees.

Heart's spirits lifted when she saw the trees.

She turned in a slow circle, looking up the mountain slopes. They were dotted with trees halfway up—and the trees thickened into forest above that.

Heart hummed as she did her work. Soon Moonsilver could be outside the wagon during the day.

Heart cut grass for Moonsilver. "You'll have to be inside the wagon until we leave town," she told him. "But there are forests up ahead where the trees will hide you."

He nuzzled her cheek and she had to stretch up to hug him.

Heart brushed Avamir's milky coat until it shone.

Then she helped gather firewood.

But while she worked, her pulse beat in rhythm to her thoughts.

The gates had to mean something important. Who had made them? The man Tibbs was looking for?

Heart shivered.

Maybe *he* would know something about her family.

The silver bracelet on her wrist seemed to tighten for an instant.

Heart caught her breath.

She set down the firewood she was carrying and slipped her shawl off her shoulders. Then she pushed up her sleeve to stare at the lacy silver threads.

Would it tighten again?

She waited.

Nothing happened. She shook her head and picked up the load of firewood.

"Are you finished?"

Startled, Heart turned to see Tibbs. "Almost."

"Binney says it's all right if we walk back into town," he said. "I told her we wanted to look at the books."

Heart nodded. It was the truth—just not the whole truth.

"Binney said to be polite and kind," Tibbs said.

Heart nodded. Binney always said that.

"She says to be back before dark, too," Tibbs added.

Heart set the firewood near the cookfire. Then she walked with Tibbs back up the road. They walked fast.

It would soon be dark.

"Look," Tibbs said, pointing.

A woman was coming out of the stone building, carrying a stack of books.

She leaned to one side, trying to pull the gate closed. Heart saw the books slide and fall to the ground.

She and Tibbs helped pick up the scattered books.

"Thank you, thank you," the woman said. "Will you please pull the gate shut for me?"

Then she straightened.

She looked at them more carefully.

She frowned.

"My name is Heart, and this is Tibbs," Heart said politely. "I'm learning to read. May I please look at some of your books?"

The woman glared at her. "These books are not for just *anyone* to use," she said coldly. "They are kept here for Lord Irmaedith and his court."

Tibbs cleared his throat. "May I ask you about the gates?"

The woman's eyebrows arched upward. "The gates," she echoed.

Tibbs nodded.

"They show the ancient symbol of the Royal House of Avamir," the woman said tersely. "They are very old."

Heart blinked. The *Royal House of Avamir?*

That was her name, the name Ruth Oakes had given her. Heart Avamir.

Ruth had gotten tired of Simon calling her "girl."

Heart had needed a name, so Ruth had given her one. Heart had never thought about where the name had come from.

When the unicorn mare had needed a name, Ruth had suggested that Heart could share her own.

So she had.

Heart took a deep breath, trying to choose one question out of the dozens in her mind.

Tibbs spoke before she could.

"Ma'am?" He gestured at the beautiful metalwork. "Do you know who made them?"

The woman narrowed her eyes. "Have you never heard of Joseph Lequire?"

Tibbs leaned toward her. "Is his forge near here?"

The woman clicked her tongue and stepped back. "What business is it of yours?"

She glared at them, then turned and walked away without looking back.

Heart stood very still, her thoughts swirling like an uncertain wind.

The slow clopping of hoofbeats made her look up.

Coming through the twilight was a boy leading a big bay horse. It reminded her of the one she had seen outside Yolen's Crossing.

This one had armor as bright as lightning, blue-silver and flawless. The metal covered its flanks and sides, its neck, even its head. There were tall plumes that nodded from its forehead.

"What lord do you serve?" Tibbs asked politely as the boy passed.

The boy looked startled. "This is young Irmaedith's mount. We came for new armor." He pointed up the mountainside to the north. "The forge is a long walk from here, but we can't rest yet. I must hurry onward tonight. The parade's next week, you know."

"Parade?" Heart asked.

"The old lord died last week." The boy spat in the dirt and glared at them the way the woman had.

Heart saw his eyes stop on her shawl, then her Gypsy belt.

"Gypsies." He said it coldly, and then he walked on.

✦CHAPTER SEVEN

"What will you do?" Heart asked, walking back. The moon was rising, steady and bright.

Tibbs squared his shoulders. "I'll find his forge. I'll convince him to teach me somehow."

Heart took a deep breath. "You will leave the Gypsies?"

Tibbs nodded. "I have to. Binney will understand."

Heart knew he was right.

And she knew that she ought to go with him.

The symbol of the Royal House of Avamir had been embroidered into her baby blanket.

What did that mean?

What *could* that mean?

Surely the blacksmith who had made the gates would know something.

Binney was still awake, sitting close to the fire. Almost everyone else had gone to bed.

"I've heard of the forge," she said when Tibbs was finished talking. "I have never seen it. Nor will you," she added.

Tibbs frowned. "Why not?"

"Because Joseph Lequire works only for lords and ladies. For *royalty*."

Heart glanced at Tibbs, then back at Binney. "I have to go with him."

Trembling, Heart explained what the woman had said about the gates, about the blanket she'd been found in, about the name Ruth had given her.

Binney shook her head. "Heart. Tibbs. You are both chasing dreams you cannot catch. No one but Gypsies will take in runaways."

Heart felt tears swell into her eyes.

"What will become of the unicorns? Think of the danger, Heart!"

Heart wiped her eyes. She pressed her lips together.

She loved Binney and she knew the old woman

was trying to protect her. And she was afraid to leave the Gypsies.

But Moonsilver hated living inside a wagon.

He *hated* it.

"I have to find my family," Heart told Binney. "They will help me."

Binney shook her head. "How do you know this House of Avamir has anything to do with you?"

Heart looked to the side. She didn't know. Maybe Lord Dunraven's book would tell her, but she couldn't read it yet.

She clenched her fists and stood up.

Binney stood and hugged her. "You think about it overnight. Don't decide when you are tired and upset."

She turned to hug Tibbs. He was startled. "Consider this long and hard," she said. "You have a place with us now."

They both watched Binney walk away, then faced each other.

"I have to go let Moonsilver out," Heart said.

Tibbs walked beside her. "Binney loves you," he said. "She just doesn't want to see you hurt."

Heart didn't know what to say.

"You should stay with the Gypsies, Heart."

She nodded slowly. Maybe he was right.

"I will never tell the secret, Heart," he said solemnly. "Never."

Heart knew he meant it. "Thank you for teaching me the letters."

"You know all the sounds now," Tibbs told her. "Keep practicing and you'll get good at it."

They stopped by the wagon.

Heart opened the back and Moonsilver came out. She put her hand on his silky shoulder.

He was shivering, eager to run free. He touched his muzzle to Avamir's, then he was gone, galloping in the dark.

"Good night, then," Tibbs said quietly. He smiled at Heart and took her hand for a moment. Then he headed back toward Davey's wagon to sleep.

Heart looked up at the sparkling stars.

She didn't want to be in a wagon tonight any

more than Moonsilver did. It was chilly, but the stars were spectacular.

Moonsilver cantered in long, sweeping circles.

Avamir grazed.

Heart decided to sleep beneath the sky. It was a beautiful night and she didn't want to talk to Binney just now.

She needed to *think*.

She ran to Binney's wagon for her carry-sack and her blanket.

"I'm going to sleep close to Moonsilver," she told Binney.

Binney nodded. "Take the spare blanket. Good night, dear Heart."

"Good night, Binney," Heart answered.

Happy to be outside, Heart settled herself by the wagon. Kip curled up beside her, snuggling. Avamir lay down close. Heart stared at the stars, thinking.

Moonsilver finally plunged to a stop, breathing hard. He lowered his head to eat the grass Heart had cut for him earlier.

Heart held Lord Dunraven's book in her hands.

Maybe she should ask Tibbs to read it to her before he left.

Heart took a deep breath.

She didn't *want* anyone else to read it. Whatever it said about her family belonged to her.

"And it might only tell about the blacksmith," she whispered. "Maybe the whole book is about him."

She sighed.

Zim had managed to read only five words, "The Mountains of the Moon." And that was probably wrong. It made no sense.

The sound of careful footsteps caught her attention.

Heart hid the book beneath the blanket.

She closed her eyes almost all the way shut.

Kip woke and got to his feet, staring into the darkness.

It was Tibbs, walking very quietly.

Heart opened her eyes a tiny bit. Tibbs had his things in a carry-sack. He was *leaving*.

Kip saw who it was and didn't bark. Avamir

lifted her head and Moonsilver stopped eating to look at him.

"She loves you all," Tibbs whispered to the unicorns and Kip. "Take care of her. I have to find Joseph Lequire now."

Avamir lifted her head sharply.

"Be still!" Tibbs breathed.

The mare shifted. Heart felt warm breath on her cheek. Avamir stood up and stamped one forehoof. She made a low sound in her throat.

Moonsilver looked at Tibbs.

"Don't wake her," Tibbs whispered. "And take good care of her, please."

Avamir nudged Heart so hard that she sat up, startled and angry. Tibbs started to apologize. Avamir pushed at Heart again.

Heart scrambled to her feet, gathering up the blanket so that it hid the book she was holding.

"I'm sorry," Tibbs said again. "I didn't mean to—"

"Are you leaving tonight?" Heart asked. She took a step toward him.

Tibbs nodded. "I have to, Heart."

Avamir came up behind Heart and pushed at her from behind.

Heart stumbled forward, barely hanging onto the book and the blanket.

Avamir pushed her again.

Heart faced the mare. "Do you want to go with him?"

Avamir stamped a hoof. She reached out to touch Tibbs's face. Then she pushed at Heart once more, gently this time.

"All right," Heart said aloud. "Binney will understand."

Avamir raised her head and Moonsilver pranced in a circle.

Kip sat while Heart packed her things.

She turned her back to wrap the book in a skirt.

She folded Binney's blanket carefully and laid it on the driver's bench.

Kip whined softly, but he stayed at Heart's heels as they walked away from the wagons.

✦CHAPTER EIGHT

The road up the mountain was narrow and very steep. The unicorns walked behind Heart and Tibbs.

Kip stayed beside Heart, whimpering a little, but not falling behind.

It got colder and colder as they walked.

Then it got warmer.

"This is strange," Heart said, pulling off her shawl. "It's usually colder up high."

Tibbs nodded, looking puzzled.

Heart stopped to look up the steep trail and blinked.

She caught Tibbs's sleeve. "Look."

Tibbs stopped to stare. "What is that?" he whispered.

Heart could only shake her head.

There was a weird yellow-orange light coming over the top of the ridge. It looked like the sun was rising, but the sky was still too dark for it to be dawn.

Impatient, Avamir stepped around them. Moonsilver followed.

Heart glanced at Tibbs. He hitched his carry-sack higher on his shoulder.

"Oh, Tibbs, *look*," Heart breathed as they topped the ridge.

There was a crack in the earth.

It was deep and narrow, and at the bottom of it ran a river of fiery liquid.

Avamir broke into a canter. She leaped the fissure. Moonsilver jumped right behind her. They galloped along the far side, their hooves barely touching the stone. The orange-red glow gilded their coats.

"Is that a house?" Tibbs pointed.

Heart squinted in the strange light from the river of fire.

There was a round door, like the ones in the village, set into solid rock.

Avamir and Moonsilver were cantering straight toward it.

Heart spotted a bridge across the glowing crack in the earth.

Tibbs had already seen it, she realized. He was heading toward it. She ran a few paces to catch up.

Kip didn't want to cross.

Heart finally tied her carry-sack over her shoulder and picked him up.

On the far side he scrambled free and ran ahead.

"Has Avamir been here before?" Tibbs asked Heart as they ran to catch up.

"I don't know," Heart told him.

Avamir climbed the rocky path that led to the door.

She struck it lightly with one forehoof.

"Don't!" Heart pleaded, running to catch up. "Let us talk to the blacksmith while you hide."

Avamir struck the door a second time.

"At least tell Moonsilver to hide," Heart pleaded with the mare.

She saw Tibbs looking at her and realized how silly she must sound, arguing with an animal.

"She can understand you," he said. It wasn't a question.

Heart nodded. "I think she must. Usually she does what I ask, but . . ."

The sound of the door opening stopped her words.

Heart stared.

A tall man with fierce eyes was looking down at them. "Who dares to beat on my door?" he demanded. Then he saw Moonsilver and Avamir and fell silent.

"I have come to beg you to teach me the craft of my heart," Tibbs said.

"And I have come to ask if you know anything about my family," Heart managed to add.

The man rubbed his eyes and shook his head. Then he laughed. "Well, come in, then. All of you."

Heart followed the others up the steep path, glancing back at the river of fire.

It seemed to end at the base of the hill.

As she passed through the round door, she saw that it didn't.

It ran through the lowest room of Joseph Lequire's house.

"Sit down and rest yourselves," the smith said, leading them upstairs. The unicorns went first, graceful on the stairs. Kip followed.

Heart and Tibbs sank into chairs.

Heart had never touched anything so soft.

Kip sat at her feet, panting. He was trembling, and she patted his head.

Avamir and Moonsilver stood quietly beside them.

Heart was amazed at the room. It was huge. The ceiling was so far overhead it felt like a starless sky. There were paintings on the walls and thick carpets on the floor.

It was as fine as Dunraven's castle had been. The soft fiery light filled the room.

The smith kept staring at the unicorns.

"They are real, then?" he finally murmured.

He looked at Heart and Tibbs. "My family has long worked this forge. Its heat makes our work impossible to match."

Avamir shook her mane.

The smith smiled. "There is a family story. It claims a unicorn touched the ground with its horn to open the forge fire. I never thought it was true."

Avamir tossed her head.

The smith laughed. "The story says we owe them a favor, should ever they ask." He smiled. "I suspect I am being asked this night."

"Do you know anything about the House of Avamir?" Heart asked.

He shook his head. "I do not."

Heart felt her eyes sting.

The smith rose to his feet. "But perhaps I can help you some other way." He faced Avamir. "M'lady, my skills are yours."

He looked at Heart and Tibbs.

Heart leaned close to Avamir. "I came to ask him about the book," she whispered, "and about finding my family."

Avamir turned her head.

Heart squirmed, turning all the way around in the chair. "We can't go on hiding Moonsilver forever and—"

Heart stared at Avamir, confused.

The mare was facing the wall.

Heart lifted her eyes to the paintings.

The one Avamir was looking at showed a horse wearing silvery armor.

Heart caught her breath.

"I think she wants you to make Moonsilver something like that." Heart pointed at the painting. "Then he won't have to hide all the time."

The smith nodded. "It will take two or three days. It has to fit perfectly."

"Did you make the gates in town?" Tibbs asked. "At the library?"

Tibbs shook his head at the unfamiliar word.

"The place with all the books," the smith said.

Tibbs nodded.

"No," the smith said. "My great grandfather did. And he used a design from *his* great grandfather.

We all bear the same name—it gets passed down."

His face sank into sadness. "I have no son. Others have passed the name to an apprentice, but I am forbidden to have one until I am old."

Tibbs made a sound of despair.

The smith scowled angrily. "Lord Irmaedith was afraid an apprentice might take the family secrets to another lord's lands. Now he is gone. His son may be wiser."

"I was born to work metal," Tibbs said softly. "It is in my heart and blood. I *dream* about it."

The smith smiled broadly. "You sound like a true smith. Shall we see?"

"You'll let me work with you?" Tibbs asked eagerly.

"M'lady unicorn wants armor for her son," the smith said. "I can use your help. I've just made armor for the new Lord Irmaedith. His highness the unicorn shall have even finer."

Moonsilver stood straight and tall, arching his neck.

Tibbs joined the smith in laughing.

Together they went down the stairs.

Heart watched them go, feeling the weariness of the long walk creeping over her.

Then she realized something and jumped up.

"Will the unicorns be safe here?" she called down the stairs.

The smith looked up. "Yes. No one comes into the forge without my permission."

"Then I will be back tomorrow night," Heart said. "I'll go ask the Gypsies to wait."

The smith raised a hand in farewell.

He picked up a hammer and turned to a pile shining silver metal.

Tibbs looked at Heart. "Alone?"

Heart smiled. "Kip will come."

Tibbs hesitated, giving her time to change her mind. When she didn't, he smiled. "We will make a beautiful disguise for Moonsilver."

Heart called to Kip.

Together they went out the door into the gray light of dawn.

✦CHAPTER NINE

Heart's spirits were so high she nearly ran down the path as the sun rose.

Even though the smith knew nothing about her family, everything would soon be better.

Moonsilver would be able to graze and gallop freely. He could travel with the Gypsies without bringing them—or himself—danger.

Heart hummed a flute tune.

Kip chased rabbits, then came racing back.

Coming around the last curve in the path, Heart was smiling.

Binney would be so glad to see her.

Davey would be too, and Zim, and . . .

Heart heard shouting and stumbled to a halt.

The voices were loud, angry.

Kip stayed close as she crept forward.

She hid, peeking out to see.

There were dark-shirted guards surrounding the Gypsy wagons.

The guards were the ones shouting.

Binney and Zim stood close together.

Binney looked old and pale, her hair still mussed from sleep.

The rest of the Gypsies were breaking camp.

The children were hushed.

There was no singing or laughter this morning.

Heart could see Binney talking to one of the guards.

He turned his horse away, shaking his fist at her. "You'll go to Bidenfast because our young lord commands it. That's all you need to know, old woman!"

Heart stared, her eyes stinging.

If she ran to help, the guards wouldn't let her leave. She wouldn't be able to return to the forge for the unicorns.

Angry, helpless, she could only watch as Binney was pushed along toward her wagon.

Bidenfast.

Heart repeated the town's name so she would remember. She would follow as soon as she could.

There was nothing else she could do.

"Kip?" she whispered.

He scrambled after her as she turned and made her way back up the rocky path.